Copyright © 2009 Jenny Alexander
Illustrations copyright © 2009 Mark Oliver
Reading ~~consultant~~ MA, PhD

First published in Great Britain in 2009
by Hodder Children's Books

1

A Catalogue record for this book is available
from the British Library

ISBN 978 0 340 98148 1 (HB)
ISBN 978 0 340 98154 2 (PB)

Typeset by Tony Fleetwood

Printed and bound in Great Britain by
Clays Ltd St Ives plc, Bungay, Suffolk

The paper and board used in this book is a natural recyclable product
made from wood grown in sustainable forests.

Hodder Children's Books
a division of Hachette Children's Books
338 Euston Road, London NW1 3BH
An Hachette UK company
www.hachette.co.uk

CAR-MAD JACK
JACK
The Marvellous Minibus

Written by
JENNY ALEXANDER

Illustrated by
MARK OLIVER

Hodder
Children's
Books

A division of Hachette Children's Books

· CHAPTER 1 ·

Car-mad Jack loves Saturday mornings.

First, he wakes up. He remembers what day it is — and smiles!

Then, he has breakfast. He goes to the car supermarket — and smiles!

Then, he chooses a great car to play in. He has an exciting adventure. He makes a poster — and he smile-smile-smiles!

But one Saturday morning there didn't seem to be any great cars to play in. There were just lots of middle-size family cars and a boring minibus like the one they had at school. Jack felt as sad as someone who found nothing in his Christmas stocking but a measly bag of crisps.

'I don't think I'll play in the cars today,' he said.

Dad was surprised. 'What about this Ford Escort?' he said. 'It's a very nice car.'

Jack shrugged. 'It isn't the kind of car you could have an adventure in.'

Dad suggested three or four other cars but they all looked boring and ordinary to Jack.

'I might go inside and do some drawing,' he said.

They went into the showroom together. Jack had his own drawer in Dad's desk where he kept his pencils, pens and paper.

He had a big display board called 'Jack's
Wall of Cars' where he stuck up all his
posters. But he couldn't make a poster
today.

The point of posters was to make the
customers want to buy the cars. Posters
had to make the cars sound exciting. Jack
couldn't stick up a poster that said 'Boring
bus' or 'Ordinary Escort'.

He decided to tidy up his drawer instead.
He emptied everything out on to the table.
He put all the good sheets of paper back
in a tidy pile and the crumpled ones in the
recycling bin.

Jack sharpened all his colouring pencils.
He went through his felt-tip pens. He threw
all the ones that had gone dry in the bin.
After that, he didn't know what to do. It

wasn't a normal Saturday morning. For the first time ever at the car supermarket, Jack felt bored.

Dad was in the office going through the post with Mrs Merridew. Jack looked out of the big windows at the cars. Maybe there was one he could have an adventure in, even if it wasn't a very exciting adventure. Then he saw something that made his eyes light up. It wasn't a sports car or a van or a four-wheel drive – it was Granny Bright!

She was wearing her favourite green sandals and a yellow dress covered in big purple flowers. There was a new pink stripe in her light brown hair. 'Bright by name and bright by nature!' That's what everyone said about Granny Bright.

She burst through the glass doors and

Jack ran to give her a hug.

'What are you doing here?' he cried. He had never seen Granny Bright at the car supermarket before.

'Your dad asked me to come and have a look at his palm tree. He tells me it's gone droopy,' she said.

Dad heard Granny Bright's loud cheerful voice and came out of the office to say hello.

'Thank you for coming,' he said.

'You're welcome,' said Granny Bright. 'Now, where is this poor palm tree?'

Granny Bright was brilliant at looking after plants and flowers. She talked to them as if they were people. She said they told her their problems.

The droopy palm tree was standing in
a big pot at the back of the showroom. It
usually had pride of place at the front, but
Dad had moved it. He said it might upset
the customers.

The droopy palm tree looked very sorry
for itself. When Granny Bright saw it, she
shook her head.

'You are not a happy bunny,' she said.

She stroked its leaves. She prodded the
dark soil in the pot. She peered into the
saucer underneath the pot. Then she
stood up.

'Do you know what's wrong with it?' asked Dad.

'Yes, I do,' said Granny Bright. 'But before we talk about this poor palm tree, I see someone else around here is feeling a bit droopy today.'

She looked at Jack. 'What's wrong, pet?' she asked. 'I don't usually see you when I drop in at the car supermarket because you're always busy playing in the cars.'

Jack told her there weren't any exciting cars to play in today. There were no sports cars, vans or off-roaders, just boring old family cars.

'Show me!' said Granny Bright.

Jack, Dad and Granny Bright went outside for a stroll among the cars.

'See what I mean?' asked Jack.

Granny Bright nodded.

'Hmm ... This isn't the most exciting batch of cars you've ever had,' she agreed. 'But wait a minute! What about that minibus?'

She marched across the forecourt towards it. Jack had to run to keep up.

'Buses are boring,' he said.

Granny Bright stopped in her tracks. She looked shocked.

'Boring?' she cried. 'Imagine if we had a minibus like this one in the Golden Years Gardening Club. It would be marvellous! We could go on trips. We could visit all the best gardens. We could see the Eden Project!'

'What is the Eden Project?' asked Jack.

Granny Bright said the Eden Project was

a fabulous garden built in an old quarry
in Cornwall. It had huge domes called
biomes. One was always hot and steamy
like the rain forest. One was warm and dry
like Greece and Spain.

'You can see coconuts and bananas
growing on palm trees in the rain forest
biome,' she said. 'You can see lemons and

olives in the other one. That would be a really exciting adventure for me!'

They all walked over to the minibus. Just as they got there, Mrs Merridew appeared at the back door of the office. 'Who would like some coffee and banana muffins?' she called out

Dad nodded. Granny Bright nodded. Jack looked at the minibus.

'I might stay out here for a little while,' he said.

Dad grinned at him. He opened the driver's door.

'See you later,' he said.

· CHAPTER 2 ·

Jack climbed up into the minibus. He sat
in the driver's seat. He put his hands on the
big steering wheel and took a deep breath.
Then he closed his eyes for a few moments,
imagining.

Jack imagined he was parked outside the
hall in Albert Street where the Golden Years
Gardening Club held their meetings. It was
very early in the morning. The sun was
just coming up and the birds were starting
to sing.

Bus-driver Jack had come to take
Granny Bright and her friends on a day
trip to the Eden Project in their marvellous
new minibus. The minibus had 'Golden
Years Gardening Club' painted on the side,
in a ring of red roses and yellow daffodils.

The door of the hall opened and Granny
Bright stepped out into the pale sunshine,
followed by her friends. They stood on the

pavement, admiring their new minibus. Everyone was happy and excited. Jack jumped down from the driver's seat to help them climb aboard.

The first one to get on the bus was Granny Bright's best friend, Joanie. She couldn't hear very well. She wore a pink hearing-aid but it didn't always work.

'Hello, Joanie,' said bus-driver Jack, in a nice loud voice. 'Mind you don't slip.'

Joanie nodded and smiled. 'Yes, I am looking forward to the trip!' she said.

The next one to get on was Granny Bright's next-door neighbour, Frank. He couldn't see very well. He carried a white stick. He peered at Jack through his very thick glasses and said, 'Excuse me, Miss – is this our minibus?'

'Yes, and I'm your driver,' said Jack. 'Let me help you aboard.'

After Joanie and Frank came the three Simpson sisters. They ran the teashop on the corner of Granny Bright's road. It had frilly tablecloths and china cups and

saucers. It had bowls filled with little white cubes of sugar, and cake stands with silver handles.

The Simpson sisters were wearing matching cardigans with pearl buttons. They had wispy white hair, pinned back. They were chat-chat-chattering so much that they barely noticed Jack helping them up into the bus.

'So I asked him to jolly well mind his language … !' said Grace to Mary-Jane.

'Young people today!' said Mary-Jane to Ellen.

'What has happened to Mr Manners?' declared Ellen. Then she noticed Jack. He was helping her up the high step.

'Thank you, young Jack!' she said.

'Maybe Mr Manners is still alive and

well after all,' said Mary-Jane, as they chat-chat-chattered their way to the back of the minibus.

An old man with big whiskers came next, and then a woman in a floppy green hat. After them, there was a very large lady and a very thin one, who seemed to be best friends. Last of all came Granny Bright. She looked as perky as a parrot with her pink hair, purple dress and green sandals.

Jack got into the driver's seat. The two seats next to him were empty so he had the front of the bus to himself. Granny Bright was in the seat behind. She twisted round to talk to the others.

'It's a long way to the Eden Project,' she said. 'But we've got a lovely driver and I'm sure he'll get us there as quickly as possible.'

The quickest way to Cornwall was on the motorway. Jack drove straight out of town. He felt very high up, driving the bus. He could look down on the roofs of all the cars. He could see over the fences and hedges. He came to the big roundabout and followed the blue motorway signs.

Jack liked driving on the motorway. It was fast and easy. He could do a steady seventy miles an hour.

'We'll soon get to Cornwall at this rate,'
he thought.

But before they had gone very far,
the whiskery man said, 'Are we nearly
there yet?'

'How did you get your hair wet?' asked
Joanie, fiddling with her hearing aid.

'Can we stop for a cup of tea soon?' asked Frank.

'Ooh, yes. That would be nice!' chorused the Simpson sisters.

'Tea and cake!' agreed the floppy hat woman.

Granny Bright said, 'Look, Jack! We're just coming up to some services!'

Jack pulled over on to the slip road. He

drove into the huge car park and found a space quite close to the entrance.

Jack looked at the clock on the dashboard. It was ten o'clock. They would never get to Cornwall at this rate!

'This had better be a short stop, back at half past,' he said.

'Meet in the shop at half past,' muttered Joanie to herself, fiddling with her hearing aid, but no one heard her. They were all too busy getting off the bus.

In the cafe area the Simpson sisters held up the queue by chat-chat-chattering about the cakes.

'Why do they have to wrap everything in plastic?' cried Ellen.

'It's a crime against cake!' Grace agreed.

'We should speak to the manager!'

declared Mary-Jane.

Jack herded his Golden Years gardeners along the cake counter and through the pay points. He felt like a shepherd herding his sheep. He got them all sitting down at the tables and sat down with them to enjoy his

lemonade and chocolate-covered Swiss roll.

When it was nearly half past ten, Jack tapped his watch with his finger to remind them of the time. Some set off straight back to the bus. Others stopped at the toilet first.

Joanie wandered off into the shop. She waited for the others to come. She waited for ages! Then she noticed a magazine in the display that had a picture of the Eden Project on the front. She took it down and opened it. She began to read.

Outside in the bus, Jack looked at the clock on the dashboard. It was after half past. Everyone was sitting in different places so they would have someone new to talk to. No one noticed that Joanie wasn't there.

Jack shut the doors and started up the

engine. He eased the bus out of the parking space.

'Let's have a sing-song!' suggested Granny Bright.

· CHAPTER 3 ·

They sang 'One man went to mow' and
then 'Ten green bottles'. After that, no one
could think of any new songs so they sang
the same ones again. They sang each song
five times and then Frank said, 'Is it nearly
time for another tea stop?'

'Ooh, yes!' said the Simpson sisters. 'But
can't we get off this motorway and look
for a proper cafe where they don't wrap
everything up in plastic?'

'What is more important,' asked Jack,

'getting to Cornwall as quickly as we can, or having nice tea and cakes?'

'Tea and cakes!' they all shouted back.

Jack sighed. He turned off the motorway. He was still on a main road, but he couldn't go so fast and it was more difficult to overtake. He wasn't very happy but the Golden Years gardeners were.

'Now we can look for a nice cafe,' they said. 'We can get a decent cup of tea and cakes that don't need unwrapping!'

Soon they saw the perfect place. It was called the Hungry Hedgehog. It was set back from the road, behind a big garden with picnic tables. Jack pulled into the car park. He looked at the clock on the dashboard. It was half past eleven.

'This had better be another short stop,' he said. 'Please be back on the bus at twelve o'clock.'

The cakes in the Hungry Hedgehog were not wrapped in plastic but that was because they didn't have any cakes. All they had was biscuits and crisps.

'Now I can see why the hedgehog is hungry!' grumbled the whiskery man.

The Golden Years gardeners took their tea and biscuits outside to the picnic tables.

Granny Bright said, 'Isn't this nice? They may not have any cakes but they've got a lovely garden.'

'Yes,' said Frank. 'I can smell lavender and roses and mint. I might go on a smell quest!' Frank couldn't see very well so he loved the plants and flowers that had strong smells.

Granny Bright said, 'Just follow the hedge all the way round and you'll come back to where we are now.'

Tappety-tap went Frank's stick as he set off on his smell quest.

'Remember to come back to the bus at twelve o'clock,' Jack called after him.

Frank followed the hedge all the way round the cafe garden. He could smell lots of wonderful flowers like honeysuckle and meadowsweet wafting on the air. But then the hedge ran out.

Frank could just make out a gaping hole in the hedge. He tappety-tapped with his stick on the ground and felt a hard pebbly path going through it. He sniffed the air and caught the mossy smell of trees – and something else! It was the sweet smell of a butterfly bush, which was Frank's favourite smell in the world.

Frank wanted to find the butterfly bush and get a really good sniff of it. He peered at his watch. He brought it right up to his face. He knew he had to be back at the bus at twelve o'clock. Would he have time to go exploring?

Frank squinted at his watch through half-closed eyes. The numbers looked blurry and he couldn't make out where the hands were.

'I'll have to guess,' he thought. 'Hmm ... Well, I guess it must be about ten to twelve. So I've got plenty of time!'

He pottered happily through the gap in the hedge to look for the butterfly bush. But it was actually twelve o'clock when Frank disappeared through the hedge, and Jack was herding his Golden Years gardeners back on to the bus.

Jack didn't notice that another one had gone missing and neither did they. They were too busy fussing about choosing new places to sit so that they would have someone different to talk to. As soon as everyone was settled, Jack pulled out of the

car park and got going again.

'With a bit of luck, we won't have to stop again before we get to Cornwall,' he thought.

But the Golden Years gardeners felt cross that they still hadn't had any nice cakes. They mumbled and grumbled about it.

They asked Jack to look out for another cafe.

Jack saw lots of cafes but he pretended he hadn't noticed them in time to stop. He drove right past.

'There's a Little Chef!' cried the large lady.

'Where?' said Jack. 'Oh, bother – we seem to have missed it.'

'There's a Roadside Diner!' cried her skinny friend.

'Where?' said Jack. 'Oh, bother – missed that one too.'

Jack suggested that the best thing might be to keep going and not stop again until they arrived. There was bound to be a cafe with nice cakes at the Eden Project.

'But that's hours away,' cried the

Simpson sisters.

'It will be at this rate,' Jack muttered to himself.

Granny Bright said, 'Could we have just one more tea stop, Jack? Then everyone will be happy.'

They passed a sign that said, 'Pat's Pantry, 300 metres.' It had a picture of a steaming

teacup and a big slice of apple pie. Jack sighed. He pulled into the car park. He looked at the clock on the dashboard. It was one o'clock.

'We know,' everyone said, before he could tell them. 'We've got to be back here in half an hour!'

Pat's Pantry was full of customers so the Golden Years gardeners got their tea and cakes and then split up. The Simpson sisters

sat outside talking to Pat. They swapped recipes and stories.

'We run a tea shop,' they said. 'Have you tried putting a pinch of ginger in your rhubarb cake?'

They chat-chat-chattered and Pat chattered back. She invited them into her kitchen to taste her new recipe carrot cake that had just come out of the oven.

At half past one, Jack went back to the bus. He felt grumpy and tired. The Golden Years gardeners came back in dribs and drabs. They felt happy and tired. They straight away settled down for a snooze.

'At last,' thought Jack as he started the engine. 'Now I can put my foot down and just drive.'

· CHAPTER 4 ·

There were lots of car parks at the
Eden Project. Each one was marked by
a brightly-coloured fruit sign – plum,
banana, lime. The parking attendant
waved Jack through and he drove on into
the bus bay close to the entrance. There
was no sound from the back except sleepy
breathing and snores.

'We're here, everyone!' Jack said,
switching off the engine. He turned round.
He gasped.

He had started out with ten passengers. He counted them now – Granny Bright, the floppy hat woman, the whiskery man, the large woman and her stick-thin friend ... that only made five!

'Wake up, wake up!' said Jack. He was starting to panic. 'Where are the Simpson sisters? Where is Frank? Where is Joanie?'

'We must have left them at the last tea shop,' said Granny Bright. 'We'll have to go back and find them.'

Jack felt bad. He should have counted his passengers every time he set off after a stop. It would be horrible to be left behind. When he found the five missing gardeners, they were going to be very cross with him.

He drove back to Pat's Pantry as fast as he could. When they arrived, everyone got

out to help look for the missing gardeners.
The cafe was still full of people, but there
was no sign of the Simpson sisters, Frank or
Joanie.

Jack and his little gang of gardeners went
back outside. They didn't know what to do.
Then they heard faint voices coming from
the back of the building.

'I'm sure it's a lizard orchid!' said Mary-
Jane.

'That's very rare indeed!' said Ellen.

'Thank you for showing us, Pat,' said Grace.

Jack and the others went round the back of the cafe. They saw the Simpson sisters and Pat, crouching down near the bins. They were looking at a tall plant with ragged flowers.

'There you are!' said Granny Bright.

The Simpson sisters looked round. Grace

checked her watch.

'Oh, dear!' she said. 'We got chatting and didn't notice the time.'

'But look what we found,' added Mary-Jane.

All the gardeners admired the ragged orchid. They took pictures of it to show Frank and Joanie.

'Where are Frank and Joanie?' asked the Simpson sisters.

'We thought they were with you,' said Jack.

Granny Bright frowned. Maybe they had missed the bus too. Could they still be at the Hungry Hedgehog?

They all rushed back to the bus. If Frank and Joanie were still at the Hungry Hedgehog they would be furious with Jack by now for driving off without them. He had to get going – but there was something he needed to do first. He counted the passengers to make sure they were all on the bus.

Jack drove back to the Hungry Hedgehog. As he went into the car park, he saw Frank sitting in the garden. His white stick was leaning against his chair. There was a big bunch of flowers wrapped up in newspaper on the table in front of him.

'Stay here,' Jack said to the passengers. He jumped down out of the bus. He went over to where Frank was sitting.

'I'm so sorry for driving off without you,' he said.

'Not at all, dear boy,' said Frank. 'I must have got carried away on my smell quest.

But look what I found.'

He pointed at the bunch of flowers. He gave them a sniff.

'I bumped into the gardener and he took me on a tour. When we came to the butterfly bush he cut ten stems so that everyone in the Golden Years Gardening Club could have one.'

Jack told Frank about losing the Simpson sisters. He asked if Joanie was at the

Hungry Hedgehog with Frank. But Frank shook his head.

'Come to think of it,' he said, 'I don't remember Joanie being at the Hungry Hedgehog at all.'

Jack's heart sank. Was it possible that he had left Joanie at the very first cafe, in the motorway services? She would be as mad as a rat in a trap with him by now, if he had.

Jack carried the flowers and helped Frank go back to the bus. Everyone was delighted to see Frank, and double delighted with their butterfly flowers. Their sweet smell filled the bus.

'But where is Joanie?' they said.

'There is only one place she can be,' said Jack. 'And that's at the motorway services.'

He counted all the passengers again, to make sure no one had wandered off. Then he drove back to the motorway. He turned off at the services.

'I need a loo stop,' said the whiskery man. 'We seem to have been driving for a long time.'

Everyone else wanted to go too, so they all went in together. They passed the shop. Then they passed the cafe. In the far

corner, they saw Joanie. She was sitting in the corner having a snooze. There were five tea cups lined up on the table in front of her and a gardening magazine.

Granny Bright touched her shoulder. Joanie sighed and slowly opened her eyes.

'Wh-wh-where am I?' she mumbled. 'I was having such a lovely dream. I was at the Eden Project with all my lovely friends. Oh!' She suddenly remembered where she was.

She said to Jack, 'I went to the shop at ten thirty like you said. Nobody came, so I flicked through a magazine while I was waiting. It was all about the Eden Project. I must have been so busy reading that I didn't see you go.'

'While we're here,' said Frank, 'shall we

have some tea and cakes?'

'Or shall we find another cafe where the cakes aren't wrapped in plastic?' said the Simpson sisters.

Jack sighed.

'I suppose we might as well,' he said. 'We won't have time to go back to the Eden Project before it shuts today.'

· CHAPTER 5 ·

It was getting dark when bus-driver Jack finally pulled up outside the hall in Albert Street. He jumped down to help everybody off the bus.

'I'm sorry,' he said. 'That was a rotten trip. The only bit of the Eden Project we saw was the car park. And half of us didn't even see that!'

'Nonsense, dear boy!' exclaimed the whiskery man. 'We've had a wonderful day!'

Everyone agreed. It had been a marvellous outing, they said.

'We saw a lizard orchid,' said the Simpson sisters. 'And we took some pictures so everyone else could see it too.'

'I found a lovely smelling butterfly bush,' said Frank. 'And I got some cuttings so everyone else could smell it too.'

'I read about the Eden Project and then

had a lovely dream,' said Joanie. 'And I bought the magazine so everyone else could read about it too.'

They all shook Jack's hand.

'Thank you for driving us,' they said.

Then Mary-Jane had an idea.

'Let's go back to our tea shop and have a slap-up tea!'

'Would you like to come, Jack?' asked Grace.

Jack shook his head. He had had enough tea and cakes to last a week! He got back up into the bus. The Golden Years gardeners wandered off down the road. They disappeared round the corner, chatting happily to each other. Suddenly he wasn't Jack the minibus driver any more – he was Car-mad Jack at the car supermarket.

He jumped down from the bus and went into the showroom. Dad and Granny Bright were moving the droopy palm tree back towards its normal place beside the door.

'Did you find out what was wrong with it?' asked Jack.

Granny Bright nodded. 'And did you have an adventure in that marvellous minibus?' she asked.

Jack grinned. 'Yes,' he said. 'Now I'm going to make a poster of it.'

'Can I make a poster too?' asked Granny Bright.

Dad had to go and help a customer outside. Jack and Granny Bright got some paper, pencils and pens. They knelt down at the low table together and started to draw. They drew for ages, without talking. Granny Bright was very good at drawing. That was probably where Jack's mum got it from, and she was an art teacher.

When she had finished, Granny Bright held her poster out in front of her. She tipped her head on one side to look at it.

'My poster is for your dad,' she said. 'I hope it will remind him to stop watering his plants so much.'

She showed it to Jack. 'What do you think?' she said.

Granny Bright's poster had a picture of a palm tree that looked very sorry for itself. It had feet instead of a pot, and it was wearing socks. It was standing in a big wide puddle. A speech-bubble beside it said,

'Well, would you be happy if you had to stand around in soggy socks all day?'

Jack laughed. He held out his poster to show Granny Bright. It had a picture of the minibus. Underneath, he had written:

'Minibus. Marvellous for clubs and groups. But make sure you don't leeve people behind if you stop for tea and cakes.'

Minibus. Marvellous for clubs and groups. But make sure you don't leeve people behind if you stop for tea and cakes.

Granny Bright laughed.

'That's very good advice,' she said. 'Let's pin it up on your Wall of Cars.'

They pinned it up and then stood back to admire it.

'I wish the Golden Years Gardening Club could afford a minibus,' said Granny Bright, with a sigh.

'Don't sit around wishing!' said Jack. It was one of Granny Bright's mottoes. She grinned.

'You're right,' she said. 'If you don't try, you don't get!' That was another one of her mottoes. 'I'm going to suggest that we do some fund-raising. We could have a jumble sale. We could open our gardens to the public.'

Granny Bright said it would take a

long time to get enough money to buy
a minibus. 'By the time we do, you will
probably be grown up,' she said. 'Then you
can be our driver!'

Jack shuddered. He had had some very

scary adventures in the cars at the car supermarket. He had raced Crasher Clark in a fast Ferrari. He had been hijacked by an escaped prisoner in a rugged Range Rover. He had driven across the wild mountains of Scotland on a motorbike.

But trying to get Granny Bright and her friends down to Cornwall in a minibus – that was the scariest adventure of all!

Look out for more of Car-mad Jack's adventures in the following books:

The Speedy Sports Car
The Versatile Van
The Motorbike in the Mountains
The Taxi About Town
The Rugged Off-roader